Disney Princess

Deluxe Princess Music Player Storybook®

Rapunzel's Heroes

Reader's Digest Children's Books

New York, New York • Montréal, Québec • Bath, UK

Rapunzel's Heroes

It was a special day and Rapunzel was so happy! She, Flynn, and Maximus were heading into the kingdom to see the lanterns being released in honor of the lost princess!

Maximus wasn't happy. He didn't trust Flynn. After all, Maximus was a loyal palace horse, and Flynn was just a common thief.

But Rapunzel did her best to help the two of them get along. She taught Flynn how to scratch under the horse's chin and behind his ears. And she hoped it would work!

Rapunzel and her friends had to sneak past the palace guards, because Flynn was still wanted for stealing. Maximus did his best to hide Flynn.

Success! They were inside the kingdom gates. It was bound to be a great day.

There was so much for Rapunzel and Flynn to do! They explored the city's beautiful streets, walked in and out of the many shops, and danced at a festival honoring the kingdom's lost princess.

When Flynn saw a kitten trapped in a tree, he asked Maximus for help. Maximus still didn't trust Flynn, so when the thief tried to climb on his back, the horse bucked him off!

But then Maximus thought about it a little more—someone who tried to rescue a kitten might be a decent person. Might be. Maximus still wasn't sure.

That evening, Flynn arranged for a boat to take Rapunzel and him out to the middle of the lake. There they would have the best view of the lanterns being released. But before they left, Flynn gave Maximus an apple. Maximus whinnied happily and the boat floated off.

Later, Maximus heard a scuffle. Two palace guards had captured Flynn! And where was Rapunzel? Maximus knew he had to do something.

The horse thought of the crowd from the local pub, the Snuggly Duckling. They looked like a bunch of really mean ruffians and thugs, but Rapunzel had won them over earlier. They would do anything for her, and they would know just how to save Flynn from prison! Maximus took off and soon everyone headed to the palace.

Maximus and the others were able to release Flynn. But they still had to save Rapunzel! She had been locked in a tower because of her magical hair—it kept her cruel mother young.

The new friends no longer cared about their differences. They both wanted to rescue Rapunzel. Off they galloped!

Working together, Maximus and Flynn reached the tower. After a hard fight, Flynn cut off Rapunzel's magical hair. She could live freely now. Maximus, Flynn, and Rapunzel returned to the kingdom, safe and sound.

Best of all, Flynn and Maximus were friends, ready for even more adventures together. Rapunzel couldn't have asked for a better ending to a perfect day.